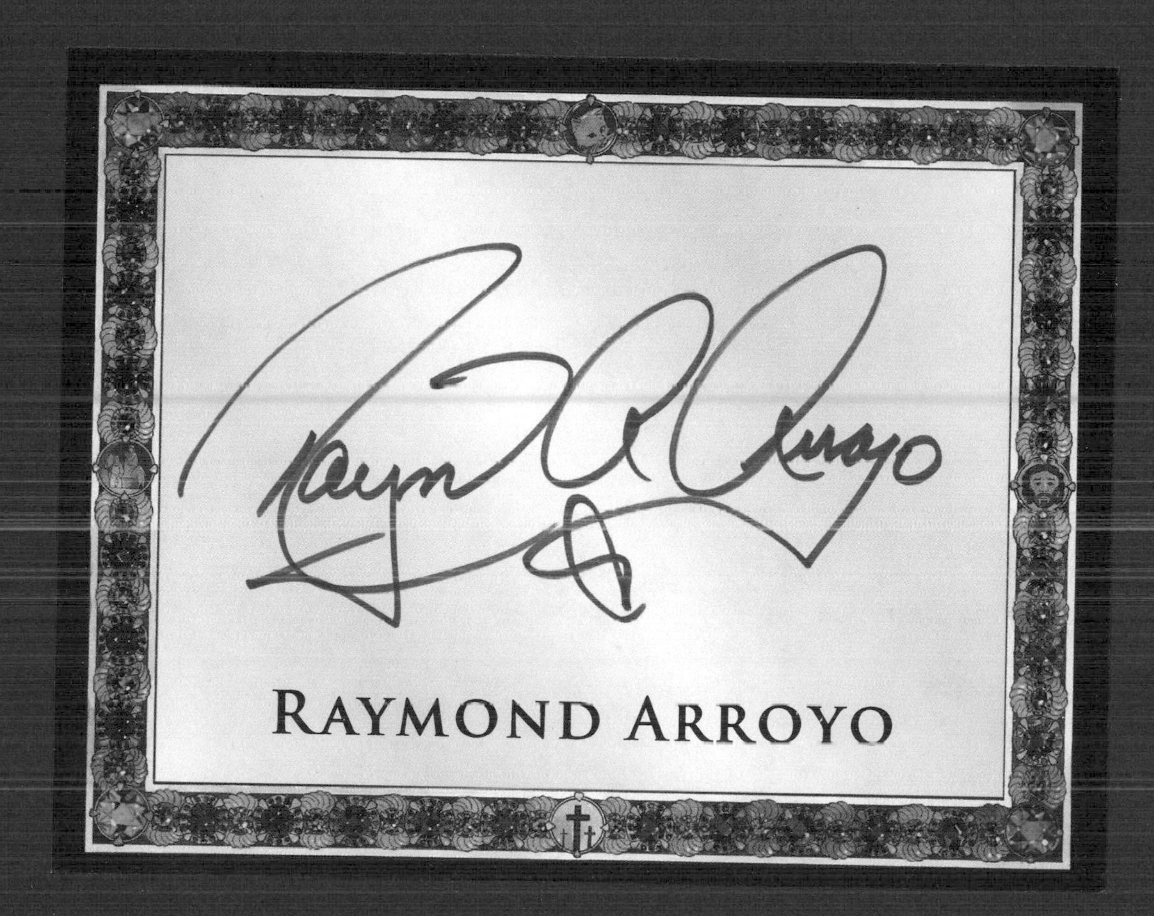
RAYMOND ARROYO

THE *Thief* WHO STOLE HEAVEN

SOPHIA
INSTITUTE PRESS

Sophia Institute Press®
Box 5284, Manchester, NH 03108
1-800-888-9344

www.SophiaInstitute.com
Sophia Institute Press® is a registered trademark of Sophia Institute.

ISBN: 978-1-64413-238-8

Library of Congress Control Number:
2020952892

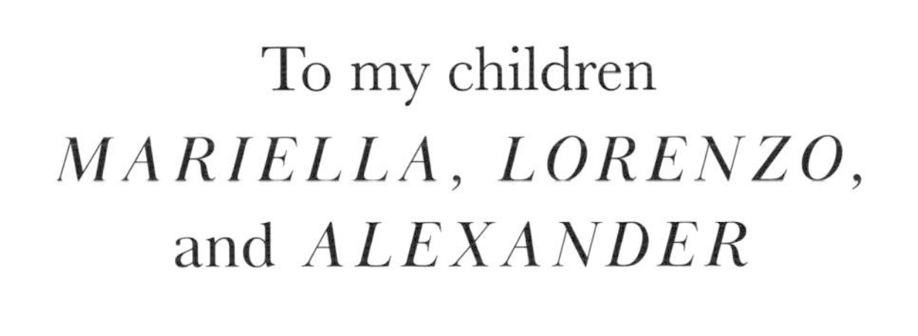

To my children
MARIELLA, *LORENZO*,
and *ALEXANDER*

And to our godchildren
DMITRI, *NIKO*, and *MARIA*

...may mercy always be theirs.

Dismas was a thief — a member of a wandering band of robbers who prowled the Judean desert looking for easy prey.

Abandoned by his parents, the boy fell into the hands of a gang that raised him in their ways.

He didn't want to steal
or hurt anyone.

But to eat — and to avoid
a beating by Gestas,
his leader — the boy
did as he was told.

And it came to pass that Dismas was ordered to rob a widow by pushing her into the street and taking her money.

Once the deed was done, the widow's kitten followed the boy into an alley where he counted the stolen coins.

Feeling guilty, he tenderly cared for the kitten as if it were his own.

When Gestas discovered Dismas feeding the tiny cat, he became furious.

"You soft idiot!" he fumed. "That thing produces nothing. Mercy is a great weakness, boy." Gestas grabbed the cat by the throat, and Dismas never saw it again.

Time hardened Dismas.

Not only did he become the most feared bandit in Judea, but he was so cruel and quick with a blade that the thieves began calling him "the Prince of Death."

Now one night, while Gestas and the others slept, Dismas spied a rich merchant on a camel bouncing down the highway. He silently slipped from the thieves' cave, carrying only his knife.

Within minutes, the merchant was no more. Dismas took charge of the camel and six small sacks of gold, which he greedily stuffed into his pockets.

The braying camel woke Gestas. "Where'd you get that creature?" asked the old thief, standing in the dark mouth of the cave.

"It came wandering by," Dismas lied. "We can sell it for a hefty price."

And behold, over a nearby hill there came a man with a lamp, leading a donkey. Atop it sat a woman tightly bundling her Baby against the cool night air.

"We are highly favored, Gestas." Dismas smiled his crooked smile, touching his blade once more. "The night brings us yet another prize."

Dismas leapt onto the highway, blocking the travelers' path.

"Welcome to my kingdom," he crowed.

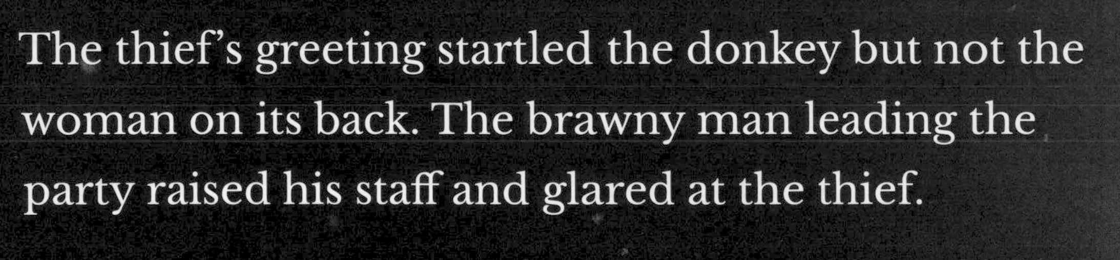

The thief's greeting startled the donkey but not the woman on its back. The brawny man leading the party raised his staff and glared at the thief.

"Save your strength," Dismas snarled, flashing his knife and going straight to the saddlebags. "What have we here?"

"Only a Child," the man responded.

"Do you think I care about you or your Child?"

Rummaging through the saddlebags, Dismas glanced up at the beautiful woman with skin like silk. She softly kissed the feet of the Infant in her arms and pressed her head against His tiny toes. Then the Child, ever so slowly...

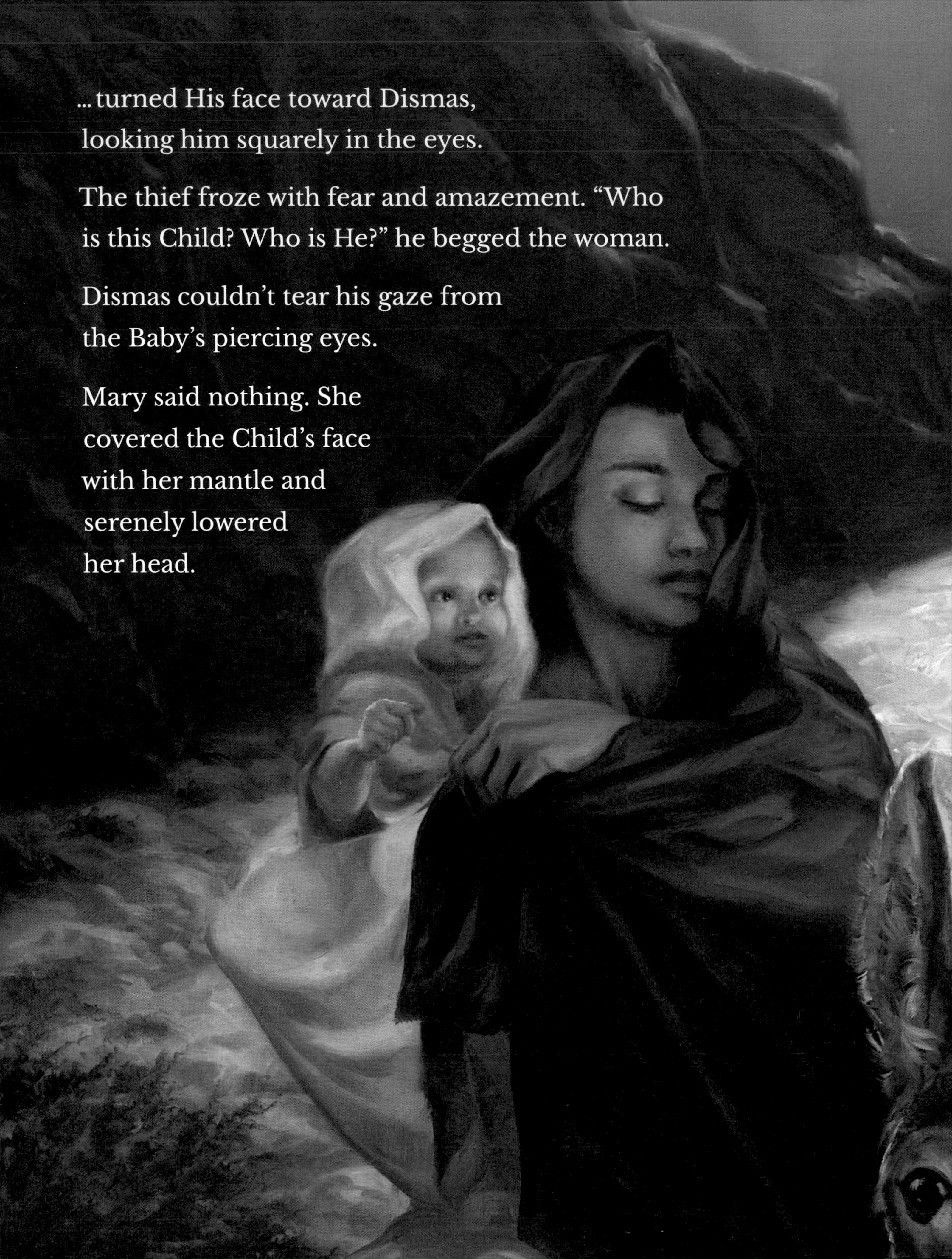

...turned His face toward Dismas, looking him squarely in the eyes.

The thief froze with fear and amazement. "Who is this Child? Who is He?" he begged the woman.

Dismas couldn't tear his gaze from the Baby's piercing eyes.

Mary said nothing. She covered the Child's face with her mantle and serenely lowered her head.

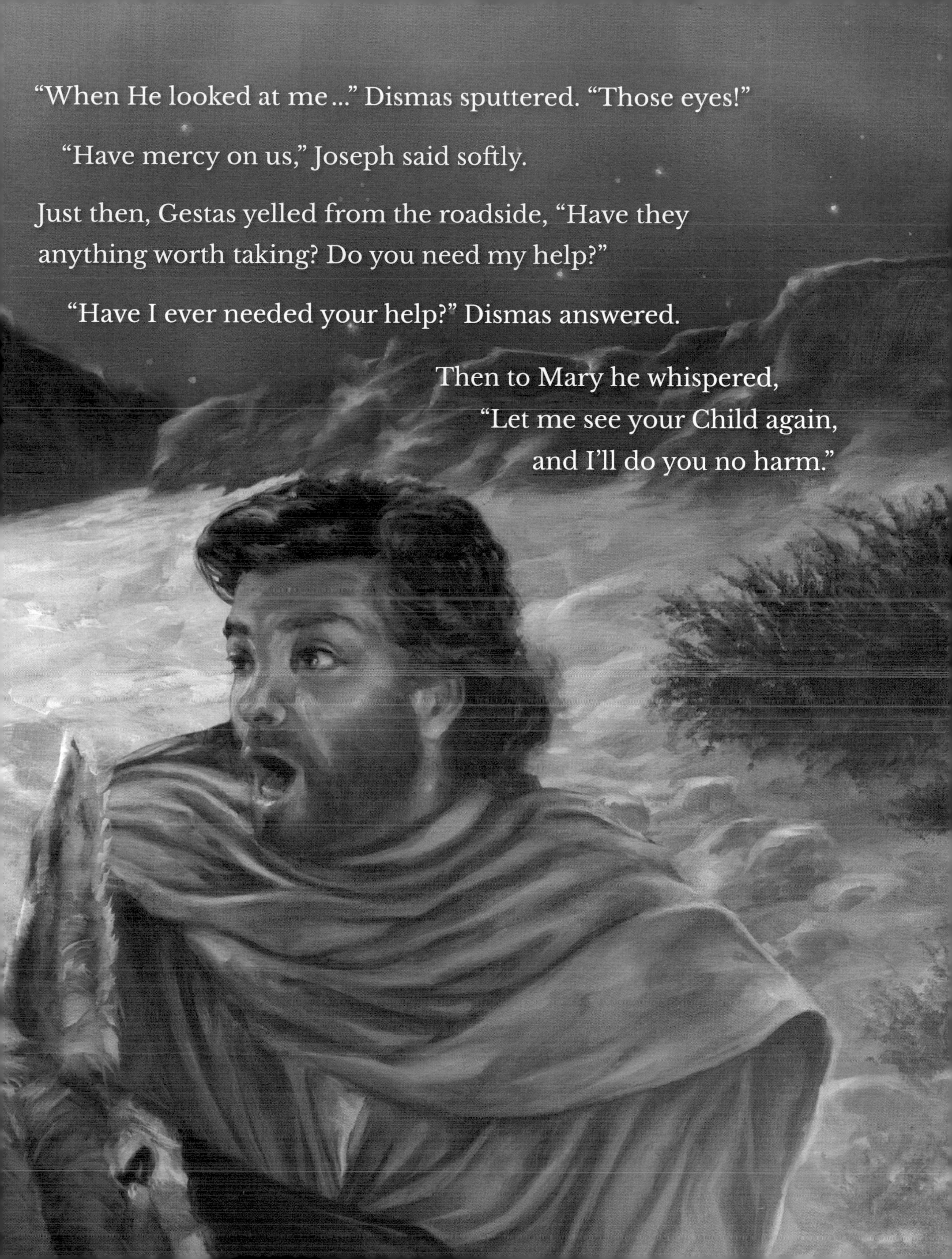

"When He looked at me..." Dismas sputtered. "Those eyes!"

"Have mercy on us," Joseph said softly.

Just then, Gestas yelled from the roadside, "Have they anything worth taking? Do you need my help?"

"Have I ever needed your help?" Dismas answered.

Then to Mary he whispered, "Let me see your Child again, and I'll do you no harm."

Mary looked to Joseph, who nodded his approval. Gently, she lifted her blue veil, and behold, the Child was already staring at Dismas alone. And He was smiling.

The thief felt such shame — shame for what he'd done, even moments ago — and amazement at the light and purity he saw in the Child's eyes.

Awestruck, Dismas stretched out his hand to touch the Baby. The Child gripped the thief's finger with the strength of a man.

Hairs bristled on Dismas' arms and at the back of his neck. He tried to pull away but could not.

In panic and wonder, he murmured to the Child, "If ever a time should come when I need your mercy, remember me."

The Babe released Dismas' finger, and Mary swaddled Him once more. "Let it be done to you according to your word," she whispered.

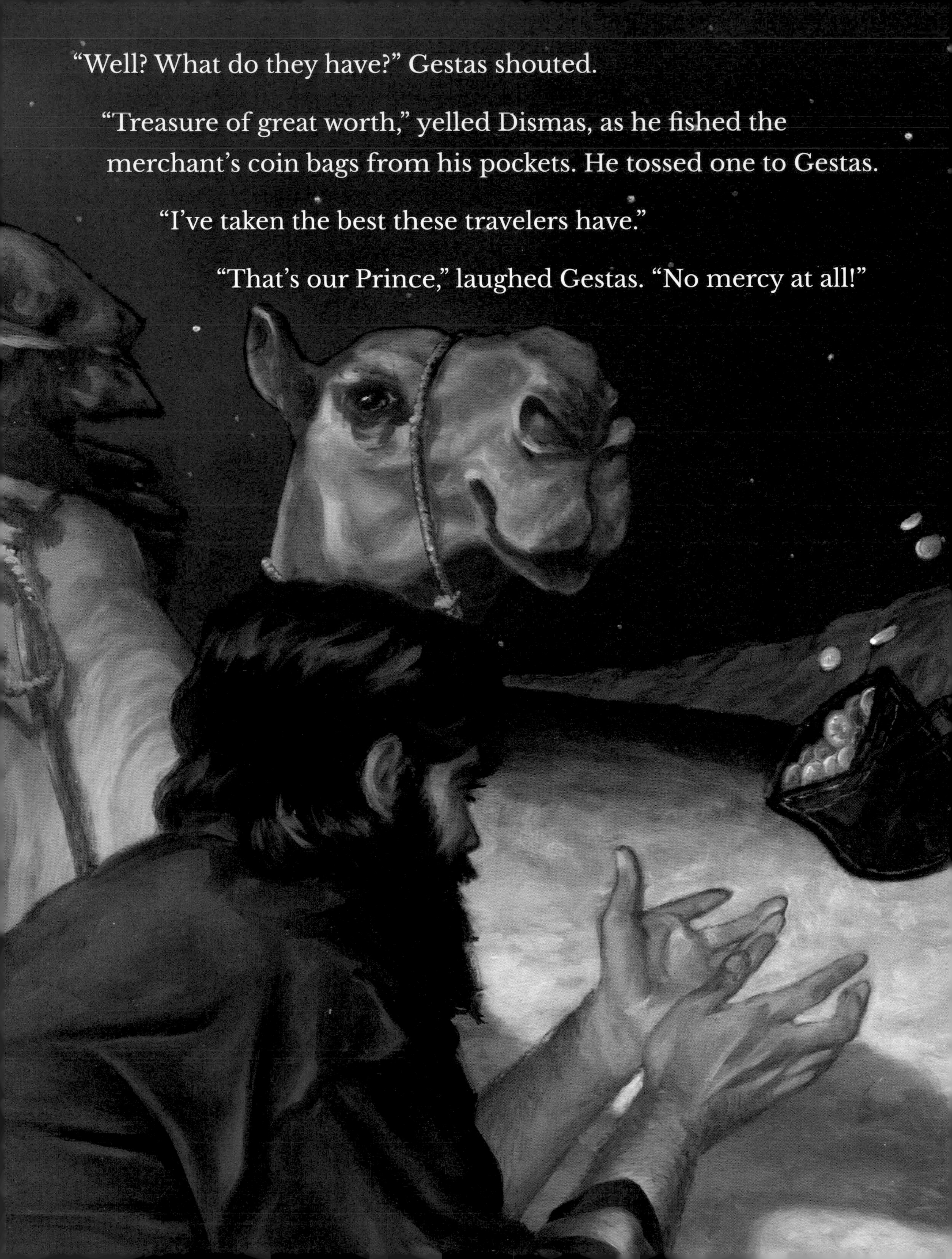

"Well? What do they have?" Gestas shouted.

"Treasure of great worth," yelled Dismas, as he fished the merchant's coin bags from his pockets. He tossed one to Gestas.

"I've taken the best these travelers have."

"That's our Prince," laughed Gestas. "No mercy at all!"

"Go now," Dismas ordered Joseph, under his breath, "Be on your way."

Then to Mary, "Do not forget what has passed this day."

She smiled at him, gently lowering her head, and the family continued down the road to Egypt.

For years thereafter, Dismas often thought of the Child he had spared on the road to Egypt.

No one had ever looked at him in such a way.

But over time, the lures of the world — gold, power, and the violence used to secure them — blotted out all memory of the Child and the bright moment they shared on that cold winter's night.

And it came to pass that Dismas descended deeper into his wicked ways. He mercilessly robbed and hurt many people, until one day, thirty-three years later, Dismas and Gestas were arrested by the Romans.

Soldiers dragged the two thieves before Pontius Pilate, the Roman governor of Judea. He sentenced them, along with another prisoner: a Preacher from Nazareth.

By the time Dismas saw the Preacher, the Roman guards had beaten Him horribly. Dismas could not believe how still, even peaceful, the Preacher remained throughout His sufferings.

The two thieves and the Preacher were forced to carry heavy crosses up the hill where they would face their final punishment.

Women on the roadside wept as the wounded Preacher passed silently by. "Jesus!" the women cried. "Rabbi! Master!"

But others screamed, “Blasphemer!
If you are the Messiah, save yourself!” and
“Where are your angels to save you now?”

“Who is this Jesus?” Dismas wondered,
dragging his cross behind the man.

“Who is He?”

On a dusty hilltop, soldiers fixed the three men to their crosses. Dismas had never known such pain. The blinding sun made it impossible for him to even open his eyes.

Then as the light shifted, the shadow of Jesus fell upon Dismas.

And for the first time on the cross, the thief could see.

A woman in a dark blue veil approached the Preacher's cross and kissed His feet. She rested her forehead against them, speaking in a hush.

Dismas knew this woman,
this mother.

He raised his glance to the face of the Preacher. Jesus was already staring at Dismas alone.

“Those eyes! You are the Child, grown!
You remember me!”

IVDAEORVM

The crowd pressed in, jeering at Jesus. "He saved others; let Him save Himself! Come down from the cross and we will believe that you are the Messiah."

The Roman soldiers mocked Jesus with false bows, threw trash at Him, and shouted, "All hail the King of the Jews! Save yourself!"

Jesus looked heavenward and Dismas heard Him say, "Father, forgive them, for they know not what they do."

Gestas, on the other side of Jesus, took up the chants of the crowd, yelling, "Are you not the Messiah? Save *yourself* and *us*!"

Shocked at Gestas, Dismas shouted back at him, "Do you not fear God? We have been rightly punished for the things we have done. We are getting what we deserve. But this man has done nothing wrong."

"You are a soft fool," Gestas shrieked. "An idiot."

Then, gazing at the innocent man next to him, beyond the bruises, Dismas suddenly saw the Child again, and all his pain vanished. Warmth filled his being.

The wicked things he had done over so many years fell away, and Dismas saw only those eyes!

"Jesus," he sobbed, "remember me when You come into Your kingdom!"

Mary smiled up at him, just as she had so long ago.

Jesus turned to Dismas and said, "Truly I tell you, this day you will be with me in Paradise."

Dismas was a thief to the end, never forgetting his trade. Before kings and prophets, apostles and saints, Dismas was the first to break through the gates of Paradise.

For hanging on a cross,
with nothing but his words and faith...
He stole Heaven from God Himself.

The Gospel of Luke contains a fleeting mention of an unnamed good "thief," who has fascinated believers for centuries. Who was he? From where did he come? And might he have encountered this Jesus before? Among the writings of the saints and Church Fathers, I discovered a trail of legends and rich insights into the character of the "good thief" — many of which I used to tell my version of his story.

There is an Arabic "Gospel of the Infancy" that, while not accepted as part of the Bible, tells of the Holy Family encountering Dismas during their flight to Egypt. Blessed Anne Catherine Emmerich records a similar vision. St. Augustine and St. Peter Damian also speak of the Holy Family being confronted by robbers during their journey to Egypt.

As for the name Dismas (which in Greek means "sunset" or "death"), it seems that it was first affixed to the good thief in the fourth-century apocryphal Gospel of Nicodemus. St. Anselm of Canterbury claims that Dismas was part of a nomadic family of thieves. St. John Chrysostom offers more detail, writing that he was a desert robber who ruthlessly killed his victims. Pope St. Gregory the Great goes further, claiming that Dismas was "guilty of blood, even his brother's blood."

The line Dismas speaks to the Child Jesus in my story is taken from St. Augustine. The saint wrote that the thief told the Infant, "O most blessed of children, if ever a time should come when I should crave Thy mercy, remember me and forget not what has passed this day."

The arc of this story is what first drew my attention: how the long shadow of grace can unexpectedly ambush even the greatest of sinners. And this may well be the first tale of Easter. After all, while the Apostles said nothing, it was Dismas, a murderer and a thief, who understood and affirmed the divinity of Christ two days before the rest of the world caught on. "To such faith," St. Augustine writes of Dismas, "what could be added? I know not, for in truth, Christ hath not found so great a faith in Israel — nay, nor in the whole world."